D1712755

Duck Therapy

Written and Illustrated by Joni Armstrong

The duck eggs had been in the incubator for twenty- eight days......
when the pecking started.

The eggs were getting little cracks and holes in them and they were pretty wiggly! "Peep, Peep, Peep" . . . little bills, little wings, and little webbed feet could be seen coming out. The ducklings popped out of the shells with a last hard push, then waddled around with their wet feathers stuck to their sides before they rested after all their hard work.

I told the children about it and they were sooooo excited! They smiled, and giggled, and laughed.

As their feathers dried, we took the ducklings out of the incubator and placed them on wood shavings in the bottom of the metal horse trough that we used as a duck nursery. They ran around peeping and eating, and then all of a sudden they would stop in their tracks and lay their little heads down for a nap.

When I told the children how cute and funny they were, they were sooooo excited! They smiled, and giggled, and laughed.

The eggs had hatched and all the silly little ducklings were under the heat lamp in the nursery . . . all but one.

There was one egg still in the incubator. It had a little crack and had been wiggling for days, but the egg just wouldn't open up. We could hear it peep, and see its little bill pecking and some downy fuzz through the crack, but no little duckling had appeared.

We watched and waited ... and watched and waited ... and watched and waited. Then the movement stopped.

Sadly, we walked away.

When I told the children, they were very sad.

The next day, while feeding the new ducklings, to our surprise we heard a loud peeping. We rushed over to the incubator and laying beside the broken egg shells with sticky wet feathers was the cutest little duckling ever!

I picked him up and held him, and after a few extra loud peeps, he snuggled right into the palm of my hand and went to sleep.

I told the children about it and they were sooooo excited!
They smiled, and giggled, and laughed.

He was tinier and weaker than the other ducklings and was sleeping so soundly that I put him in his own little box, and he slept nestled under the heat lamp against the side.

I told the children about it and they smiled, and giggled, and were very quiet as if they might wake the little duckling.

At first he couldn't stand. When he tried, his leg would kick out and flip him right over onto his back, and then he would peep extra loud with his little legs kicking in the air.

I told the children about it. They smiled, and giggled, and laughed and thought he had to be the funniest and cutest ducking of all.

I made him a little bag
filled with unpopped popcorn
that he could lean against.
Then he could stand with its support.

I told the children about it. They smiled, and giggled, and laughed at that funny little duck.

We named him CP,
which was short for
Certainly Precious.

I told the children about his name. They smiled, and giggled, and laughed, and thought it was the best nickname ever.

One of his wings was very
tiny and stuck out from
his side. The other he
held out to keep his
balance when he tried
to walk.

I told the children about it. They smiled, and giggled, and laughed, and thought he was very brave to keep trying even if it was hard.

CP couldn't walk because one of his legs stuck straight out and the other one stayed curled underneath. . . so I did his stretches several times a day.

I told the children about it, and they asked if it hurt. When I said “no”, they smiled, and giggled, and laughed that I was doing stretches on such tiny little legs.

With the stretches, CP's curled up leg uncurled and he could stand on it and hop. He didn't tip over, and he moved himself forward pretty fast.

However, his other leg stayed straight out and would not cooperate with the whole walking task, so I made a little splint out of blue craft foam to give it a nice long stretch. Sometimes I had to sneak it on while he slept, so he would be still and not wiggle out of it.

I told the children about it and they thought this was the funniest thing.
They smiled, and giggled, and laughed at CP's little blue splint.

Ducks love to swim, so I put CP in the bathroom sink and filled it. He had a hard time staying upright and tipped over in the water, so I had to help him with just one finger. He wiggled his little feet and splashed with his wings, and swam, and swam.

I told the children about it and they said that they also thought swimming was fun. They smiled, and giggled, and laughed about CP splashing in the water.

The splint and stretches worked. Soon CP could walk (still with a little hop) and followed me everywhere.

. . . into the kitchen where he got into the bottom cupboard and spilled the cereal. Apparently little ducks like Cheerios and Froot Loops!

. . . into the pantry where he ended up rolling around with the vegetables.

. . . into the toy room where
he played with all the toys.

... and into my office,
where he played with the
computer and then slept
on my lap while I worked.

I told the children about it, and they thought CP was so funny. They smiled, and giggled, and laughed, and couldn't believe that he was smart enough to use my computer.
They said they liked Froot Loops too!

Today CP took a car ride to my work.

When he followed me in, the children were sooooo excited!

They smiled, and giggled, and laughed, and thought CP was Certainly Precious

. . . and the most wonderful duck in the whole wide world.

This is a story about a real duckling, who had some challenges, did his therapy, and was Certainly Precious.

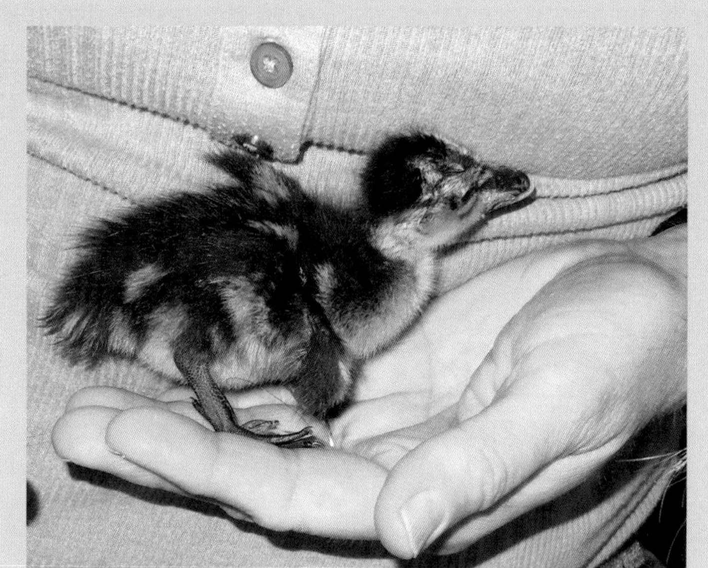
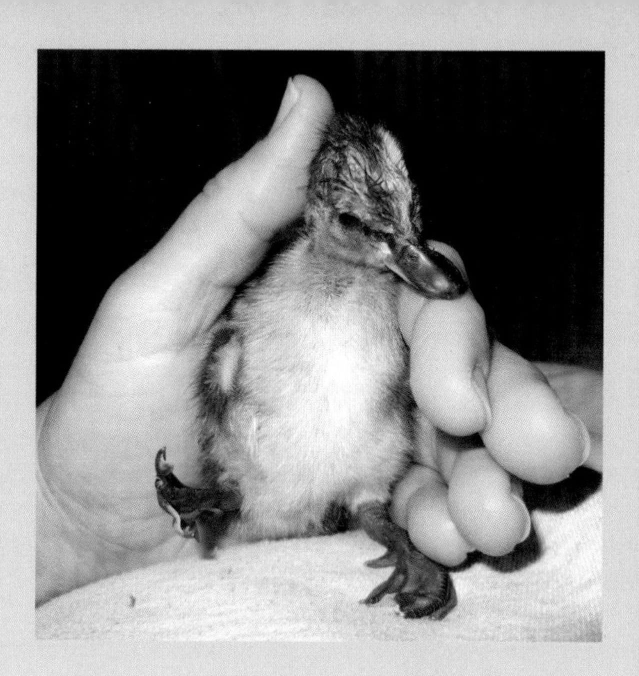

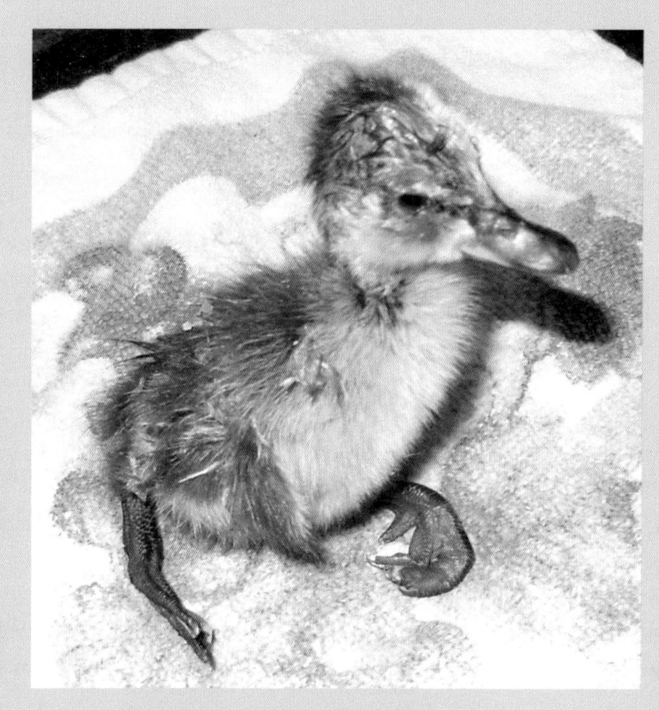

For "our kids" in therapy, who I hope gain inspiration from this story.

Thank you to my family for once again putting up with "another project".

Special thanks to Amy Johnson, whose skills on the computer helped put this book into print.

As always, thanks to God for providing fun experiences to make into wonderful stories.
To God the Glory.

Joni Armstrong

Duck Therapy

TGTG Books, 11687 Long Lake Dr. NE, Bemidji, MN 56601
jrplus4@paulbunyan.net

Printed in the United States, by Bang Printing, Brainerd, Minnesota.
ISBN: 978-0-9855299 -1-8

Cataloging in Publication Data
Armstrong, Joni
Duck Therapy / by Joni Armstrong, illustrated by Joni Armstrong – 1st Edition
Summary: A little duckling has therapy after hatching with disabilities, just like the children who enjoy his story.

Illustrations were done in pencil sketch and watercolor. The text type is Papyrus Regular.